W9-CLJ-392

Ice Queen

Exploring Icebergs and Glaciers

Imagine That!™

by
Anna Prokos

RED CHAIR PRESS

illustrated by
Jamie Meckel Tablason

Imagine That! books are produced and published by Red Chair Press

Red Chair Press LLC   PO Box 333   South Egremont, MA 01258-0333

www.redchairpress.com

 FREE Lesson Plans from Lerner eSource
and at www.redchairpress.com

Publisher's Cataloging-In-Publication Data
(Prepared by The Donohue Group, Inc.)

Names: Prokos, Anna. | Tablason, Jamie Meckel, illustrator.
Title: Ice queen : exploring icebergs and glaciers / by Anna Prokos ; illustrated by Jamie Meckel Tablason.

Description: South Egremont, MA : Red Chair Press, [2017] | Imagine that! | Interest age level: 006-009.
| Includes Fact File data, a glossary and references for additional reading. | Includes bibliographical
references and index. | Summary: "Have you ever wondered what the coldest place on Earth is like?
The coldest place on Earth is Antarctica, a large ice-covered continent at the southernmost point on the
planet. Readers will join early explorers like Henryk Bull and Roald Amundsen in exploring this icy
land and learning about the various types of glaciers and icebergs."-- Provided by publisher.

Identifiers: LCCN 2016934109 | ISBN 978-1-63440-149-4 (library hardcover) | ISBN 978-1-63440-155-5
(paperback) | ISBN 978-1-63440-161-6 (ebook)

Subjects: LCSH: Icebergs--Juvenile literature. | Glaciers--Juvenile literature. | Antarctica--Juvenile
literature. CYAC: Icebergs. | Glaciers. | Antarctica.

Classification: LCC GB2403.8 .P76 2017 (print) | LCC GB2403.8 (ebook) | DDC 551.342--dc23

Technical charts by Joe LeMonnier

Photo credits: All Shutterstock, Inc except; Page 30: Pennsylvania State University, 2012;
Page 31: Brian Kielche, 2012

First Edition by:
Red Chair Press LLC   PO Box 333   South Egremont, MA 01258-0333

Printed in the United States of America
Distributed in the U.S. by Lerner Publisher Services. www.lernerbooks.com

1116 1P CGBS17

Have you ever wondered what the coldest place on Earth is like? The coldest place on Earth is Antarctica, a large ice-covered continent at the southernmost point on the planet. It is believed that no person set foot in Antarctica until 1895. The first human-landing there is thought to be Henryk Bull, with a party from a whaling ship. In 1935 the first woman set foot there. Her name was Catherine Mikkelson, the wife of a Norwegian whaling captain. The South Pole was first reached by a Norwegian named Roald Amundsen in 1911.

Now turn the page, open your mind and imagine you're on a discovery to this icy land.

Table of Contents

Clink! Clank! Clunk! Cool ice cubes dropped into Nora's cup. One by one, they stacked to the top.

"Watch out!" her father said. "Your drink will freeze. That should be plenty of ice."

"You can never have enough ice," Nora said with a smile. She loved cold things. Cold water, cold weather, even cold pizza!

"I wish I lived in an ice castle,"
she told her dad. "I'd crunch snow cones
for breakfast and ice cream for dinner!"

6

"You have a cool imagination," Nora's dad said.

Nora stared at her ice cubes, dreaming of an icy home. "I'll carve a castle out of icebergs," she thought. Suddenly, a chill rushed to her toes. She snapped out of her daydream and into...

7

A frozen kingdom!

"It's c-c-cold out here!" she chattered. Nora looked at the miles of ice around her. "I must be in Antarctica! It's the coldest place on Earth!"

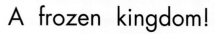

IT'S A FACT

Research stations have recorded temperatures as low as -128° F (-90° C) in Antarctica.

She shivered. Nora wasn't dressed
for the super-freezing temperature!
But she didn't mind too much.
After all, she loved ice!

Nora looked all around. Sharp, tall mountains were covered in snow. Large ice formations made strange shapes. She saw ice caves and snow sheets. There were ripples across the snowy glacier.

Some parts of the ice and snow shined bright blue. "The ice looks like it's glowing!" Nora said out loud. She had never seen anything so cool before!

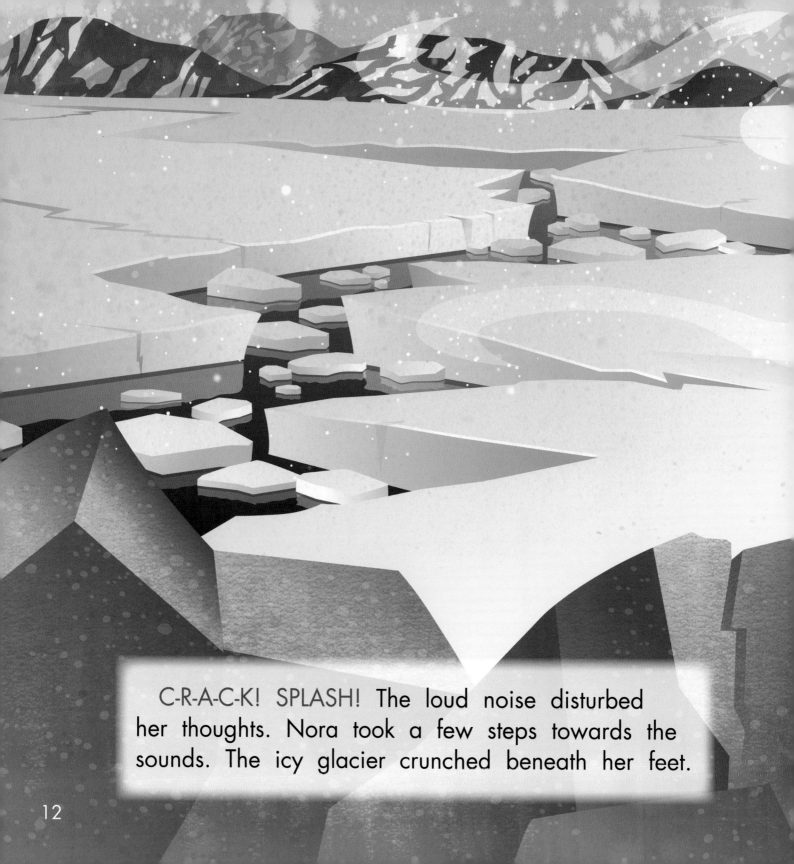

C-R-A-C-K! SPLASH! The loud noise disturbed her thoughts. Nora took a few steps towards the sounds. The icy glacier crunched beneath her feet.

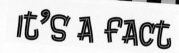
The frosty ground was filled with cracks. Some cracks were small. Many were big. Chunky ice water flowed between the **crevasses**.

Nora hopped over the cracks. She was careful not to fall in the water.

Suddenly, she heard another strange sound. This time, it was a long, loud G-R-O-A-N.

"What was that?" she wondered as she made her way closer to the sounds.

Up ahead, she saw black specks in the white snow. "They must be rocks from the nearby mountains," she observed.

But as Nora walked closer, she got a big surprise.

Those black specks were penguins!
Hundreds of them! The penguins waddled
along the edge of the ice.

They buzzed and honked. They shivered and cuddled. Some of them slid into the water. Nora watched as one penguin jumped straight out of the sea and onto...

IT'S A FACT

Penguins hunt for food near icebergs. The melting fresh water beneath a glacier attracts fish and **krill**.

"An iceberg!" Nora shouted. The giant ice mountain floated in the frigid sea. It towered above the land. The penguins looked happy on their frozen home.

"That massive iceberg would make a beautiful castle," Nora thought as she eyed the ice. She imagined how her ice castle would look. Tall and pretty and dripping with icicles.

Another groan filled the air.

"It's not a polar bear," she said. "They only live in the North Pole, not here in the South Pole. And the seals are barking, not groaning."

Where is that creaky moan coming from? Nora searched for a clue. She only saw ice, snow-capped mountains, and a few very large icebergs. "That's it!" she remembered. "It must be the icebergs!"

IT'S A FACT

Scientists have recorded the noise icebergs make as they rub against land or glaciers.

Nora could not see the other side of the iceberg—it was too big! But it looked like it slammed into the mountain.

G-R-O-A-N! C-R-A-C-K! SPLASH! Nora watched a corner of the iceberg **calve**. It cracked apart and slapped into the sea. "A mini iceberg!" Nora told the penguins. They kept on honking.

IT'S A FACT

Small icebergs less than 5 meters (16 ft) across are called growlers.

23

"Lucky birds!" Nora sighed.
"They get to live in this icy world
forever. It's my dream come true!"

"Nora? Nora!" She heard a familiar call. "Are you day-dreaming again?" She looked down at the puddle by her feet.

"The ice cubes melted as you let your imagination run wild," her dad explained.

"Oh, no!" Nora exclaimed. "That's just the tip of the iceberg!"

Breaking Up is Hard to Do!

Scientists study icebergs for clues as to what causes an ice shelf to collapse. Ice shelves are huge floating sheets of ice that connect to a land mass. Most ice shelves on Earth are along the coast of Antarctica. But the northern coast of Canada is home to several large ice shelves as well.

Scientists think that recent ice shelf collapses are related to climate change. Most of the rapidly retreating ice shelves in Antarctica are located on the Antarctic Peninsula. The Antarctic Peninsula juts north towards South America, into warmer waters. The peninsula has warmed 2.5 degrees Celsius (4.5 degrees Fahrenheit) since 1950, making it one of the fastest-warming places on Earth.

Scientists attributed rapid ice shelf collapse to warmer air and water temperatures, as well as increased melt on the ice shelf surface.

Since 1995, the Larsen Ice Shelf has lost nearly 85% of its former size in a series of break-ups.

At nearly the size of Spain, the Ross Ice Shelf is the biggest floating ice mass on Earth.

26

Antarctica Ice Shelves

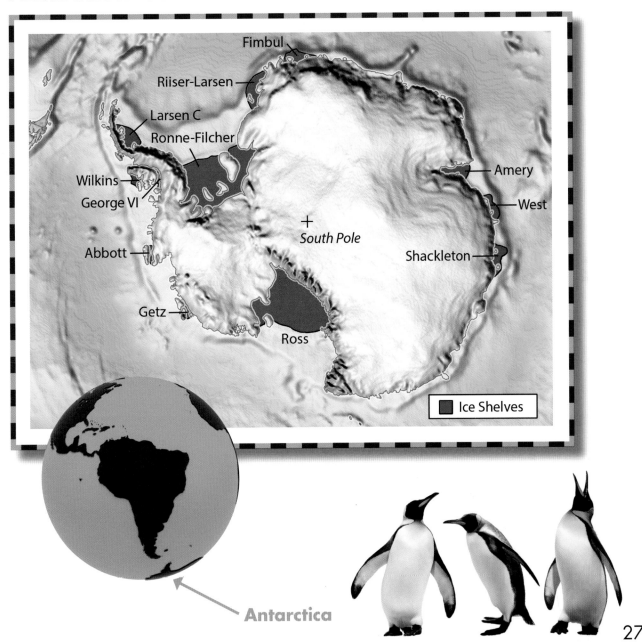

Fimbul

Riiser-Larsen

Larsen C

Ronne-Filcher

Wilkins

George VI

Abbott

Getz

Ross

South Pole

Amery

West

Shackleton

Ice Shelves

Antarctica

Going to Class on Icebergs

There are 6 official classifications for icebergs.

The smallest are called **growlers**, they are smaller than a car. Next is the **bergy bit**. These are about the size of a house. The other four are **small, medium, large,** and **very large** (it seems scientists got bored coming up with new names).

A very large iceberg is anything more than 240 feet high and 670 feet long. The largest iceberg ever found by the U.S. National Ice Center is one that broke off the Ross Ice Shelf in Antarctica in 2000. Called Iceberg B-15, it was about a half-mile thick and the size of the state of Connecticut in area!

Tabular icebergs have steep sides and are flat on top. **Non-tabular icebergs** are in a variety of shapes. Wind and water erode and carve these icebergs into beautiful shapes, like castles.

Growlers

Bergy Bits

Tabular Iceberg

Non-Tabular Iceberg

Did You Know?

About 7/8ths or 90 percent of an iceberg is below the waterline! Only a small part of an iceberg is visible above the water.

What do you think someone means when using the expression "that's just the tip of the iceberg"?

Melting icebergs cause sea levels to rise.

Fiction. Icebergs are already floating in the ocean, so melting will not raise sea level. Melting of land-based ice (such as glaciers) will raise sea level.

29

Glacier or Iceberg?
What is the Difference?

Glaciers are made of fallen snow that, over many years, become large, thick ice masses. Glaciers form when snow remains in one location long enough to change into ice. What makes glaciers unique is their ability to move. Due to sheer mass, glaciers flow like very slow rivers. Some glaciers are as small as football fields, while others grow in mountain ranges to be hundreds of miles long.

Presently, glaciers occupy about 10 percent of the world's total land area, and can be found on every continent except Australia. Glaciers can be thought of as remnants from the last Ice Age, when ice covered nearly 32 percent of the land, and 30 percent of the oceans.

Icebergs are large chunks of ice that calve, or break apart from ice masses at the ocean's edge, such as glaciers and ice sheets.

A colony of Adélie penguins on an iceberg

The Commonwealth Glacier is one of the most-studied glaciers in Antarctica.

30

As the Suess Glacier reaches the ocean in Antarctica, icebergs begin to calve.

krill

Words to Keep

calve: as a verb; when an iceberg breaks apart from a larger mass, such as an ice shelf, glacier, or iceberg.

crevasse: a deep open crack, as in a glacier or ice mass.

krill: a small shrimp-like animal of the sea, eaten by whales and penguins

Learn More at the Library

Books

Cerullo, Mary; Bill Cutsinger, photograher. *Life Under Ice.* Tillbury House, 2006.

Harrison, David L. *Glaciers: Natures Icy Caps.* Boyds Mill Press, 2006.

Petersen, Christine. *Learning About Antarctica* (Searchlight Books). Lerner Publications, 2016.

Simon, Seymour. *Icebergs and Glaciers.* HarperCollins, 1999.

Web Sites

National Geographic Education
http://education.nationalgeographic.com/encyclopedia/iceberg/

National Snow and Ice Data Center: All about Glaciers
https://nsidc.org/cryosphere/glaciers/

National Snow and Ice Data Center: Iceberg Quick Facts
https://nsidc.org/cryosphere/quickfacts/icebergs.html

Index